HAMBONE

By Caroline Fairless

Illustrated by Wendy Edelson

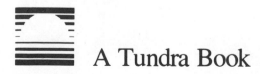 A Tundra Book

To John Larrow

Hambone © 1980, Caroline Fairless

ISBN 0-912766-97-2

Published in the United States by
Tundra Books of Northern New York
Plattsburgh, New York 12901

Published in Canada by
Tundra Books of Montreal
Montreal, Quebec   H3A 1G3

Jacket art and design by Wendy Edelson,
Lavender Moon Studio, Montpelier, Vermont

Printed in the United States

y name is Jeremy. My Papa is a farmer. Papa's farm isn't as big as the Daryl Hawkins farm, or even old Stu Hammill's. But they've each got two hired men. All Papa's got outside is my brother Alec and me, and thirty-eight Holsteins that have to be milked twice a day.

Every morning I'm up at 5:15 to help with the milking. My sister Stoner used to do it. That meant I could stay in bed till six. Then I'd get up to feed the rooster and the hens and gather the eggs.

But the rooster didn't like me, and I didn't like him. He'd peck and scratch at my legs, even through my jeans. Mrs. Grayson next door once told me it looked like I'd been running through her rose bushes.

So Stoner and I traded jobs. Now she gets the chickens and I get the heifers.

I like Thursdays. Papa picks me up at noon from Bristol Elementary. I go home to help with whatever needs it. The other kids in my class think I'm lucky. But they don't have the chores that I do.

It's the same every Thursday. Going home early gives me a chance to play with the piglets before I go with Papa to Blue Tag Grains to pick up milk replacer for the calves.

"Jeremy!" Every week Papa shouts to me through the milk-room door, "Leave those pigs alone and climb in the truck!"

We sold most of the piglets, but we still have two left. I'm not going to name them this time.

Neither one of them will be a pig like Hambone.

Hambone didn't care about anything except eating and playing with me. Ramona once told me he'd squeal when my school bus was as far away as the S-curve on the River Road. That's at least half a mile. Hambone always knew which bus was mine, because he let the first three go by without even a grunt.

After school, I'd go straight to his pen and romp with him until he was tired. Then I'd start my homework, Hambone sprawled in the clean hay, me using his back and shoulders for a pillow.

The new piglets don't care if I have to leave with Papa. But Hambone used to get mad and nip me when he heard Papa call.

Papa's a good farmer. That's what I hear at Blue Tag Grains.

"Is your Papa teaching you his planting magic?" Mr. Chamberlain asks me most every Thursday. Then he turns to the men at the counter and says, "This boy's Papa turns his fields to gold."

Papa's friends nod their heads. The summer people smile. The summer people come to Vermont after school's out in June and go home in September. They look different, stiff like toy soldiers. Their pants are clean and their shirts are new.

I like it when they talk about Papa. I remember how the farm looked when we first came from down country. And I remember what they said about it. That the farm was gone — it was land that could be developed. If Papa showed any sense at all, he could make a lot of money.

But Papa said he'd farm it, all two hundred acres. And he did. There was no magic about it. Papa worked hard. So did we — Alec, Ramona, Stoner and I. Mama was there, too, at first.

Alec is nineteen. He's the oldest, except for Papa and Ramona. I don't know how old Ramona is — she looks older than Mama. Ramona's been here since we first came. She helped Mama cook and clean. She planted the garden. Then, when Mama left, Ramona stayed.

Next comes my sister Stoner. She'll be seventeen in a month, and then she's only got one more year of high school. And last comes me. It'll be years before I even get to high school. Everybody calls me "baby" and they laugh when they say it.

Except for Ramona. She doesn't laugh. When she calls me "baby" I want to hide in her lap. But she'd say I was too big and hadn't I better go help my Papa and brother. She's right, and I go. But I don't want to. Ramona knows it, too, and she smiles as I leave.

I'm supposed to do the things Alec does. I can even drive the tractors — if only they'd let me. I begged and begged Papa to teach me, and finally he did.

I sat behind the wheel and Papa stood on the bar behind me. He yelled and screamed in my ear, shouting out which levers to drop and which pedals to step on. I couldn't get it straight. The harder he yelled, the more confused I got, and I'd mess it up again.

One day Ramona watched us. "You're trying too hard, Jeremy," she said. Then she took the wheel and I stood behind.

My mouth dropped and she asked me if I was trying to catch mosquitos like the swallows do.

"YOU can drive a TRACTOR?" I asked her.

"Can I DRIVE it? Hmph. I taught your Papa a few tricks, didn't I, Richard?"

Papa laughed so hard he almost cried. Then he squeezed her leg.

"Yep," he said. "But you'd better not go spreading that around, woman, or I won't be able to show my face."

"If you can drive it," I asked her, "then why don't you help with the planting and the haying?"

"Because Ramona's got too much to do inside to be working in the fields with the men," Papa told me. "Now do you want me to teach you to drive this thing or not?"

Ramona hung onto the steering wheel for a minute like she didn't want to let go, but finally she did and I climbed back up.

One night at supper, after lessons were over, I asked Papa if I could help with the haying that summer.

"You already do help," he said.

"I don't mean help with the raking," I told him. "I mean, can I drive the tractor?"

"Nope," he said.

"Why not?" I argued. "I can do it."

"Because you aren't old enough."

"Babies don't drive tractors," said Alec.

"But I can DO it," I replied.

Papa got up from the table and went to his chair in front of the television. That was the end of the talk.

I *have* to work in the barn. Old Mean Florence is the only cow who ever kicked me, and she only did it once. She kicks everybody. Papa and Alec kick her back, but then she strikes at the heifers on either side. I sing the songs that Mama taught me, and that settles her down.

Florence is off her milk now, and soon she won't be around to kick me again. She's been mean for as long as I can remember, and I won't mind it when she goes. But the other animals — it makes me sad when they go.

"Don't be a sissy," Alec once said. He scowls when he talks to me and puckers his eyebrows like Papa. "You get over it — you have to."

But he was wrong. I still feel it, every time. And I'll never forget Hambone.

Mrs. Erdmann, my teacher last year, asked me once why my compositions were always dirty. "Do you write them in mud puddles?" she asked me, and the kids in my class laughed.

That was Hambone, Hambone's nose. If he wanted my pencil, he'd grab for it. Whatever was on the end of his snout — cabbage, egg shells, spinach — showed up on my composition. Mrs. Erdmann was reading last night's supper.

Papa is like Alec about the cows. "Cows! They're just like women," he says. "Milk them till they're no good any longer and then send them off."

He laughs every time he says it, like he's teasing. Alec laughs with him. But Mama's gone. She's been gone since I was six. She's not dead. We get letters from her, every two weeks on Fridays.

She's in the city and she writes us about the sidewalk hot dog carts — I'd eat myself sick, she says — and the boats in the harbor. And the music... music everywhere!

Alec doesn't read her letters. He folds his arms across his chest and says he has no Mama.

Stoner reads them out loud to me. I try to picture the sidewalks and the subways and the pigeons, but I can't.

One time after Stoner read Mama's letter, she said maybe we

ought to write Mama back, that Mama'd probably be glad to hear from us. I grabbed the letter and tore it to bits.

"NO!" I shouted. "We're not going to write her. Not now. Not ever!"

I wanted to kick something, or pound something. I slammed my bedroom door. The empty milk glass on the dresser rattled but didn't fall, so I opened the door and slammed it again. This time the glass crashed to the floor and I felt better.

"You act just like Alec," said Stoner.

I didn't answer.

"Mama's happy," she said. "That counts for something!"

"Mama can't even drive a tractor!" I yelled across the room.

Stoner didn't say a word after that. She just walked out.

I remember Mama. I remember her fingernails.

"Didn't Mama have long fingernails?" I asked Stoner once.

"Yep."

I thought so. That's what I remember. At night, when Mama'd come to tuck me in bed, she'd scratch my back and tickle my arms with her fingernails and tell me about the city and her music and how she used to play.

"But Mama, you could play here," I'd tell her.

She'd scratch my head and sing to me.

"Sing to Pridey too," I reminded her once. Mama gave me the poster of the lion that hangs over my bed.

Mama smiled and sang to us both while I fell asleep.

Ramona wants Papa to marry her. "The children's Mama has been gone long enough," she says, "and people will talk."

Papa says, "Let them talk."

Sometimes I wonder what will happen when Ramona stops being good. I don't want Papa to send her off, like he did Mama and the cows. Twice I tried to tell her that.

"Ramona," I wanted to say. "Ramona. You're good and you better keep on that way or you'll be sent away like Mama was."

I only get as far as "Ramona, you're good..." before I got scared and went to the fridge for something to eat, like I was saying her cooking was good.

I was afraid Papa would walk in and I know how mad he gets when he sees me scared. Besides, I don't think Papa sent Mama away. I think it was Mama who left. Only no one ever comes right out with it.

But none of this is what I want to tell you. I want to tell you about my garden and the tomato memorial for Hambone.

I was never allowed to work in the garden.

"Girls plant gardens," Alec told me.

I've planted before, corn every year. But that's for the cows.

I'm talking about the kind of garden that grows weeds you have to pull and where the rabbits and woodchucks come for lettuce.

I thought there was enough in the garden to spare for the ground hogs, but Papa said no, and told me to shoot the ones that dug under the fence.

I'd sit at the edge, real still, with Alec's Winchester across my knees, and watch Ramona and Stoner with the hoe and the mulch.

Stoner has big muscles for a girl. She can heave a bale of hay from the wagon to the loft. I liked to watch her chop weeds with the hoe.

If I was quiet, I could hear Stoner's secrets. Timmy Hedlund asked her to the Bristol A-Fair. Mr. Parrish, who teaches science, told

14

her to apply to the College of Agriculture at the University — that she could major in Plant and Soil Sciences — and did Ramona think Papa would let her?

Sometimes a ground hog would plow through the grass to the fence, nose in the air, sniffing for good things to eat. I'd take aim and shoot. But I'd always shoot just a bit above his head.

The noise would scare him off. Ramona and Stoner would laugh and laugh as they watched him scurry away. I'd go to the barn and tell Papa, "Just got me another one... big one, too. One shot, right in the head. Tossed him into the river."

I'd stand in front of Papa with one hand on my hip, like Alec does, and try to look casual. Papa'd scratch his head through his cap, then tell me to get back to the fields with Alec.

But the ground hogs still ate the garden. One day Alec came to sit with me. Papa may have told him to. Hunting is what Alec likes to do best. Most every weekend he's off in the woods with his gun by himself. So he settled right in beside me, in no hurry to get back to work.

I prayed and prayed that no ground hog would show up, but sure enough one did. I could see the hay split and then come back up long before he reached the garden. It was easy to follow his trail.

I tried to get Alec to look in another direction, but he saw the ground hog, too.

"Git your gun ready," he said and pointed.

I didn't know what to do. I couldn't shoot him. I started to sweat and shake. I aimed at the point where he'd come out of the hay... thinking and thinking. I had to do something.

Suddenly, just as I knew he'd be coming out, I threw the Winchester in the air and yelled as loud as I could, "I'm bit! Something's bit me!"

I ripped off my shirt and rubbed and scratched a spot on my belly until it looked red and angry. The ground hog lumbered off, and I laughed inside. But it didn't work. Alec knew. He grabbed me by the neck and shoulders and shoved me toward the barn.

"Fool!" he yelled. "Idiot!"

From then on Alec kept the ground hogs out. I'd hear the shots and bite my teeth and try to think of something else.

Once he killed a big one and had it stuffed. He was proud of that ground hog. It sat on the table next to his hunting magazines and his gun books. I have to go through Alec's room to get to the bathroom, but I look away so I don't have to see it.

One winter I asked Papa if I could help in the garden when it came time to plant.

"You're more like a girl than the girls," Alec said.

Papa laughed. "My son the ground-hog slayer," he said. "If you take care of the garden like you take care of the ground hogs, we'll be eating weed pies for supper."

Then he stopped laughing. "No, you can't work in the garden," he said. "You'll work with Alec. And don't ask me that again."

I stayed with Ramona that night while she washed the dishes. She told me that Papa needed my help more than she and Stoner did.

"But I can help Papa and work in the garden too," I argued.

Ramona took a big breath and pulled her hair off her face with her soapy hands. "You do what your Papa tells you to do," she said.

That spring I found a magazine with pictures of vegetables and seeds for sale. I read it to Hambone and showed him the pictures, but he tried to eat it. From then on I kept it under my mattress.

One night I was looking at the pictures and Stoner came in without knocking. I tried to hide it. I thought it was Alec.

But Stoner listens to me and explains things without making me feel bad or stupid like Alec does. So I showed her my treasure.

"If I had a garden," I said to Stoner, whispering so Alec couldn't hear, "I'd pull the weeds out, one by one. I'd plant a little extra for the ground hogs. And I'd talk to the plants and ask them real softly to grow big... the BIGGEST anybody ever saw so nobody can laugh at me."

"I don't laugh at you, Jeremy," she said.

Stoner looked a little like Mama that night, except for her fingernails. Stoner's are short. But she looked at me like Mama used to, and her eyes were soft like Mama's.

I told Stoner that when I grew up I would have a farm with vegetables and flowers, maybe apple and cherry trees. But no cows, because then I won't have to kill them. No cows, no chickens, and no pigs.

"Except for Hambone," I said. "Hambone will be president — President of the Garden."

Stoner laughed. "Jeremy," she said softly, "somebody has to kill the cows and the chickens. We've got to eat. Every time you eat a hamburger or a drumstick, it means that something has been killed."

"NO!" I yelled and covered my ears.

I know it's true what Stoner says. But it isn't the same. Hamburgers don't look like cows. And bacon doesn't look like pigs. It's different when it's already on the table. It has to be.

I started to cry, so Stoner stopped talking about the killing. She went to the mirror and fooled with her hair. She piled it on top of her head, like Mama used to do, to see how it looked. At least she didn't laugh.

Then she turned around and said, "Besides, you love the animals. You love to play with them and talk to them and feed them. You're the best of all of us in the barn, you know. Isn't that right?"

It's true. I love them. And I AM the best.

Papa tells me I'm wasting my time and his, talking to the animals and patting them. He's begun to make me help with the butchering. I don't like it but I try not to show it. I'm not big enough to do much

anyway. I'm pretty short for my age. Alec sometimes calls me "The Runt" and it makes me mad.

"Get The Runt to carry the milk pails," he'll say to Papa when he knows I'm listening. "Tell The Runt to throw more hay down."

Sometimes I'd like to jump on him, straight down through the hay chute. But I don't.

I told Stoner that night that I would have other kinds of animals on my farm. "Lions and bears. Zebras, and maybe even a grouchy old alligator."

"And Hambone," Stoner added.

I laughed. "And Hambone."

Stoner looked at me for a long time. She didn't say a word. Then, real quiet, she whispered, "Jeremy, I'll tell you what. If Papa says you can, I'll give you part of my garden and you can plant anything you want in it, okay?"

I sat up and shouted.

"Sh-h-h," said Stoner.

I covered my mouth and lay back down. I was frightened and excited at the same time. I hugged Stoner because I couldn't say anything.

She fluffed my pillows like Mama used to do and kissed me goodnight.

 was the last one to breakfast the next morning.

Everything looked the same. Papa had his stack of bills and receipts in front of his plate. As he ate, he read the figures to Alec who added them up on the pocket computer.

Ramona moved from the stove to the table, cooking and carrying oatmeal, sausage, waffles and eggs. Stoner was still half asleep, but she sat at her place by the toaster and put in the bread.

The television was giving the morning farm report and the weather.

Everything looked the same, but something had changed during the night.

I sat in my chair next to Ramona's empty one. I buttered my toast and tried to think of a good way to ask Papa about Stoner's garden. I couldn't think of one. I was ready to blurt it out when Papa said, "Jeremy, we're doing Hambone in today and I want you out there

21

with Alec and me in fifteen minutes.''

There was silence in the kitchen. No one moved.

''Hambone?'' I said.

''You heard me right.''

Hambone... I heard the words that Papa said. And my own words stuck in my throat.

I stared at Papa and then at Alec. They both watched me. Then the words came out. ''Nope,'' I said. ''I'm not going to be there.''

It surprised me as much as anyone. I shook so hard my teeth knocked up and down. I heard Stoner suck in her breath, and then I heard nothing. Silence can be louder than shouting.

I knew I wasn't going out there, not even to say goodbye to Hambone. I loved him too much.

Papa pushed his chair back. It scraped against the floor. He came to stand in front of me — he seemed to move like a slowed-down toy. I thought he might hit me, but he didn't. He just stared.

Then right after that Stoner said, ''He's not going out to the barn because he has to help me plant the garden this morning.''

My mouth dropped. My body felt weak, and I could hardly hold my head up. Papa was breathing hard, like he'd been running. He ran his hand over his face. He did it again. Then he turned and left for the barn. Just as he started through the screen door, I saw his shoulders drop and I nearly cried out.

I'd seen shoulders do that once before, on a 'coon caught last winter in the teeth of Alec's fox trap. Alec usually checks his traps alone. He usually does everything alone. But that Saturday morning he woke me early and said I could come with him.

It rained the night before and then froze, so the snow was covered with a crust. It crunched under our feet as we walked.

The sun was out and it was a beautiful morning. Then we heard the thrashing, still a long way off, and all of a sudden I didn't want to be there.

When we first saw the 'coon, his back was up and curved and he was fighting to get free. But as we got close, suddenly his back came down like a balloon with the air leaking out. He gave up.

Alec shot him quickly, before I could stop him.

"Why?" I cried. "He's no fox. Why did you go and shoot him?"

"Oh, Jeremy. He'd have died with his foot torn through like that."

"Maybe not... just MAYBE NOT!"

"Jeremy! Stop being such a baby!"

That was the end of it. But I couldn't eat the stew that Ramona made that night. I can still see that 'coon, dead before he was shot. And when Papa sagged his shoulders as he walked out the screen door to the barn, I could see him again.

I wanted to stop Papa and tell him I didn't mean it. "Put your shoulders back up," I wanted to say.

But I did mean it. I wasn't going to the barn.

It seemed like hours passed before I dared to look up. Stoner looked as scared as I did. But she said real quick — her whole body shook — "Come on, Jeremy. Hurry and eat. Those seeds aren't going to plant themselves."

Eat! I couldn't eat a thing, and I told her so.

Ramona said, "Drink your milk." Ramona always tells me to drink my milk. She poured a fresh glass from the morning's milking, tasted it, and handed it to me. I drank it fast and slammed the glass on the table.

"Jeremy!" Ramona said, "Pick up that glass and put it down gently."

I picked it up and put it down *very* gently. Ramona laughed. Then I raced Stoner to the cupboard by the stove for the seeds and we headed for the garden.

"You pick and then I'll pick," I said to Stoner.

She picked beets. "They have to go in first," she explained. "They take a long time to grow."

I chose a packet of corn because I knew how to plant it.

Stoner picked peas. "I'll plant them, you shell them," she laughed.

I picked the tomato seedlings. Hambone loved tomatoes. We'd play a game. I'd bring him the bucket of slop with no tomato. Hambone would sniff at it and turn away. I'd have the tomato behind my back. If I held it there too long, Hambone would mosey to the door of his pen, turn and race back, grabbing the tomato as he flashed by.

Suddenly I began to cry and choked on my tears.

"It's Hambone, isn't it?" asked Stoner.

I nodded. "I can't help it."

All I could think about was Hambone. I used to tiptoe into the barn, drop onto my hands and knees and sneak into his pen. Hambone would wait until I was all the way inside. Then he'd charge and butt me like a goat. I'd butt him right back.

I'd growl and he'd grunt. He'd race through the little door to his outside pen and hide around the corner. I'd follow him out and pretend I didn't know where he'd gone.

Then Hambone would tear around the corner, kicking up dirt like the wind in a storm. He'd squeal and I'd laugh so hard I'd fall in the mud. When we were tired, Hambone plopped down wherever he was, his feet sticking out of the straw like the needles in Ramona's pin cushion. He'd put his snout on my lap if I was near, and dig into the straw when I had to go.

I stood in the garden and looked at the river below me, thinking about Hambone. Stoner stood next to me.

"Jeremy, Hambone has to die," she said. "It's the way things are, and you know it like I do. But I'll tell you what. You can make a memorial to Hambone. That way he'll live forever."

I didn't understand what she meant. If Hambone had to die, then he had to die. How could I fix it so he'd still live?

Stoner explained about memorials to soldiers — I learned about those in second grade — and memorials to great leaders and memorials to rich people.

"And even though the real ones are dead," she told me, "people look at the memorials and in some way, they're still living."

Stoner kept on talking and I began to understand. Something was growing inside me besides sadness.

I clapped my hands. "We'll make a tomato memorial for Hambone! Let's do it now!"

Stoner told me to dig a hole and put all the things in it Hambone liked the best.

"When the hole is full again," she said, "put the seedling in and then we'll have a memorial service."

I chose a spot in the corner of the garden closest to the river and I began to dig. It had to be a big hole. There were many things that had to go into it. When I was nearly finished Stoner came to look.

"Jeremy!" she laughed. "I think that hole's big enough for you to take a bath in!"

I grinned. I was proud of the hole. "It's for Hambone," I said. "Because he was so big."

Stoner said, "Okay. What did Hambone like the very best?"

"Tomatoes."

"Besides tomatoes."

"Rolling in the cow dung."

"Go get some and put it in the hole."

I went to the manure pile behind the barn. It was taller than me. Probably taller than Alec. I found my shovel with the sawed-off handle and dug a tunnel into the center to find some less ripe. I took out four buckets—it made no dent in the pile—and began to fill that bathtub hole back up.

Next came the pile of slop from the kitchen. Ramona had left it, like she always does, on the sink counter next to the fridge. There were cabbage leaves in it from supper the night before. Hambone liked cabbage. At least he liked it better than I do. There were egg shells in the slop, oatmeal and coffee grounds.

Ramona was sweeping the floor. She looked at me like she wanted to ask me a question when I grabbed the pail, but she didn't say anything.

"What will we do with the slop from now on?" I asked her.

Ramona leaned her broom against the wall and kissed me on the top of my head. "I guess we'll compost it until we have a new litter."

"There won't be a new litter," I said. "There won't be any more pigs."

I carried the slop to the garden and sloshed it into the hole.

"Hey, Jeremy!" Stoner called from the other end of the garden. "Do you remember the time Hambone got drunk on Alec's wine?"

Yep. I'll never forget it. Hambone had got out of his pen during the night and found the batch of wine Alec made from the dandelions I picked last year. Alec had put a balloon on the top of each bottle to let the gas build up and to keep the air out. Hambone must have bitten one of the balloons to get at the wine.

He was down for days in the toolshed, on his back, his feet in the air like he was dead, only he wasn't. I thought he was cold, so I covered him with straw. The only things showing were his snout and his feet.

"Go get that bottle," Stoner shouted. "Break it and put it in the hole."

The empty bottle was still with the others in the toolshed. I smashed it against the cement floor, swept it up into an empty grain sack and put the broken pieces into the hole.

"Hambone," I whispered, "you won't ever be cold again."

While I was getting together all of Hambone's things, I was thinking about the crazy things he did. Like the time he escaped from his pen and decided to explore the River Road. He was halfway to Bristol before Papa discovered he was gone. And he didn't want to come home. The only way Papa could get him back was in the bucket loader of the tractor. There was old Hambone, high in the air. Papa was driving down the River Road as fast as he could, and Ramona and Mrs. Grayson in the white house next door were clapping and cheering like they were in the Bristol Parade.

"What about the bone-toothed comb?" I called to Stoner.

Hambone loved to have his back and belly scratched.

"Why not?" Stoner called back.

But then I remembered. The comb was hanging on a nail in Hambone's pen.

"You'll have to get it," I said to Stoner. "It's in his pen."

Stoner stood slowly and stretched. Then she started for the barn. I watched her climb the fence at the edge of the garden.

"Stoner! No!" I cried.

She turned around.

"Don't go in there. We'll stick the comb in later."

I thought Hambone would like the red ribbon he took at the A-Fair last summer. It should have been the blue one, because Hambone looked much better than the Woods' hog. But Jack Woods wins the blue one every year, no matter what his hog looks like.

Hambone didn't care what color it was. He'd just as soon have eaten it. And would have, too, if Papa hadn't taken it away from him.

It was Papa who cared, and me too. We were mad. If it hadn't been for Mr. Grayson, Papa might have punched Jack Woods. I'd have

liked to see it.

Papa and Mr. Grayson were standing in front of the judge's stand. Jack Woods was close by.

"It should have been the blue one," I heard Papa say to Mr. Grayson.

Jack Woods heard him say it. "You'd have got it if your hog was any good," he said.

Papa glared at him for a minute. Then he walked straight for him.

There was a fight coming. Papa's fists were clenched tight to his sides. And he looked hot! As hot as I'd seen him since Alec flunked his chemistry test.

Mr. Grayson caught up to him and put his arm around Papa's shoulder. I was right behind them. When they reached Jack Woods, Papa didn't say a word. He held out his hand. Jack Woods didn't want to shake it. I think he'd rather have been punched. But he did shake it, and that was the end of it, or just about.

When we had pushed Hambone up the ramp and onto the truck, I climbed in with him. I yelled out to anyone who might have been listening, "Jack Woods fills his hogs with sewer water!"

I don't think Papa heard me. Just as well, I guess. Jack Woods had his back to me and didn't turn around. But he heard. I saw him get stiff. I hugged Hambone and laughed all the way home.

I stood at the edge of the hole with my hands in my pockets and examined its treasures.

"Stoner!" I shouted. "Will you come with me to ask Mrs. Grayson if we can have some rhubarb for the memorial? You can explain it better than me."

The Graysons came to Vermont from the city, the same city where Mama lives. They write books about wild animals. I've seen one of them. Mr. Grayson took the pictures.

Before they came, we'd helped ourselves to the asparagus and rhubarb that grew every year in their back yard. That first spring, just after they'd come, I crossed the fields to the fence and watched Mrs. Grayson hang the laundry on her line.

She said "hello" when she saw me.

I said "hello" back.

"Do you have a name?" she asked.

"Are you going to mow down your asparagus and rhubarb?" I asked her.

Mrs. Grayson's mouth dropped and then she laughed. "Earl!" she called through the back screen door. "Our young neighbor wants to know if we plan to mow down our rhubarb and asparagus."

Mr. Grayson came onto the porch. "I suppose you've been helping yourselves all these years?"

I nodded. "Every year," I said.

"Well," Mr. Grayson smiled, "then you'd better continue.

Otherwise we'll be overrun by asparagus and rhubarb."

"And burdock," I said. "Don't forget the burdock."

Stoner and I went to Mrs. Grayson's door to ask for the rhubarb.

"Of course," she said. "You know you don't have to ask." Then she folded her arms across her chest. "Wait a minute. Follow me. I've got something even better."

We followed Mrs. Grayson into her kitchen where she handed us each a rhubarb tart from the top of the stove.

"Gardening makes a person hungry," she said.

I had just about got the hole filled when Stoner reminded me to add some good planting soil. I probably would have forgotten it, I was so excited about the things Hambone loved.

I dug carefully through the pile of dirt I'd taken out of the hole to find as many earthworms as I could. I knew they'd help the memorial grow. Then I filled the hole.

All this time we hadn't heard anything or seen anything from the barn. But suddenly I knew that Hambone was dead. I looked across the house to the barn behind it. Nothing had changed. It looked the same as it had the day before. But I knew my hog was dead.

It was time to put the tomato memorial in the hole and tell Hambone goodbye. I couldn't stop my tears. I missed him already.

Stoner carried the box of tomato seedlings to the hole and asked me to choose the memorial. I looked at each one. I didn't choose the

biggest. I picked the one that looked the strongest. I planted it in the hole and tamped more dirt halfway up its stem.

Then I knelt and kissed the earth around the memorial. Stoner did the same.

Stoner said, "Hambone'll live forever."

And I said, "I love you, Hambone. Grow, tomato memorial! Grow bigger and stronger than any tomato plant that's ever grown. Grow big and strong like Hambone was big. I love you, Hambone."

The tomato plant memorial seemed to grow even as we stood there watching. All summer it was like that. If the other tomato plants grew two inches and put out four new suckers in a week, Hambone grew six inches and put out twelve new suckers in the same week. If I found six or eight new tomatoes on one plant, I found fifteen on Hambone.

Hambone was the talk of Bristol.

"This boy's got his papa's magic touch," Mr. Chamberlain told the men in the feed store when I went in for milk replacer.

Mrs. Grayson and Ramona carted two canvas chairs to the river and sat by Hambone while they drank their morning coffee.

One day Mr. Grayson crossed the field to see what all the talk was about. Papa came with him. I was in the garden when they came. Papa hadn't been to the garden all summer, and I was glad Mr. Grayson was along.

Mr. Grayson wore his fishing hat with the trout flies pinned on.

At first neither of them said a word. Mr. Grayson stood there and looked at Hambone. He pushed his hat back and scratched his forehead. Papa had a funny look on his face. I couldn't tell what it was. He was smiling and trying not to. He didn't look at me. Mr. Grayson turned to me. "Needs more water at the base," he said.

He knelt beside Hambone and ran his fingers through the dirt. "I don't believe it," he whispered. He looked up at Papa and said it again. "I don't believe it."

Then he stood. "Richard," he said. "I need a couple lengths of pipe. Maybe four feet each."

Papa and Mr. Grayson went to the toolshed and came back a few minutes later. Mr. Grayson carried the two lengths of pipe and Papa carried a sledge hammer, a pail of water, and a funnel.

Papa and I both knew not to ask Mr. Grayson questions until he felt like talking. Papa looked at me and raised his shoulders. I raised mine back. Then I laughed out loud. We'd know soon.

Mr. Grayson poked one pipe into the ground about two feet from Hambone's stem and angled it toward the middle. Papa hammered it into the ground. He left about a foot at the top. They did the same with the other pipe, from the other side. Mr. Grayson put the funnel into one pipe and picked up the pail of water.

"Hold the funnel," he told me.

Mr. Grayson poured slowly, to give the water a chance to seep into the ground. We did the same with the second pipe.

"Every few days," Mr. Grayson said, "water it that way."

Every morning, after chores and before breakfast, I raced to the garden to see what Hambone had done the night before. I checked his leaves for bugs and his stem for slugs. I pulled the weeds out one by one.

"Hambone," I'd whisper. "Hambone. Do you hear all the talk? Do you hear everyone tell me I've got Papa's magic fingers? Alec doesn't tease me. He doesn't say a word. Papa says, 'Have you watered the plant today?'

"But I haven't got any magic fingers, Hambone. Stoner and I both know that. It's you that's doing the growing. I love you, Hambone."

I had to put a chicken wire cage around Hambone to hold him up. He'd got so big that he toppled any stake as soon as I pounded it in. He was taller than me, and nearly all his big yellow blossoms had turned.

Hambone was weeks ahead of the others!

"We'll have enough canned tomatoes for the whole winter!" Ramona laughed. "Just from one plant."

"Spaghetti every night!" I cried.

But one day no one paid attention to Hambone or to me. Papa and Alec and I were just finishing up in the fields when Ramona came running across the yard. Stoner was right behind her.

"Chamberlain called!" she shouted at Papa. "There's a storm coming. Laney McGuire lost his barn in Lincoln. Part of his house, too!"

Then Papa started to bellow orders as loud as he could.

"Get the cows in! Get the chickens in! Come on, come on! Get those animals inside!"

Papa doesn't bellow like that often, so we knew it would be a bad one. I ran to the barn, but the wind was already blowing so hard I couldn't shut the double doors. The next thing I knew Alec was pushing against me and the doors both at the same time. I wondered for a

minute if he was even stronger than Papa.

"Make sure the doors are tight, Alec," Papa shouted. "Then go give Grayson a hand, and sit it out with them. We'll manage here!"

I started for the tractor out in the field where Alec had left it that morning.

"I'll get the tractor!" Ramona yelled. "Help Stoner nail down the windows in the chicken house!"

The sky was black when we started for the house. Lightning was coming our way. The pause before the deep rumbling thunder told us we still had some time, but not much. We hurried as fast as we could.

Suddenly the lights went out. The house was as black as the sky. I'm not usually afraid of storms. But I was scared of this one!

"Stoner. Get the candles!" Ramona shouted.

"Come with me, Jeremy," Stoner whispered. She grabbed my hand.

We felt our way down the long hallway. Stoner kept her hand on one wall. I kept my hand on the other. I could feel the bumps in the wallpaper.

The candles were on the top shelf of the hall closet. Stoner had to stand on her toes to reach them.

"Stoner," I said softly, "are you scared?"

"Yep."

I was, too. More so every minute.

By the time we had the candles lit in the kitchen and the living room, lightning was crackling at every window. The thunder sounded like seventy guns all being fired at once. A tree went down. It was the old oak by the river. Down with a groan and a crack like I've never heard. All of a sudden I remembered that Hambone was out there, maybe under that tree. Hambone was out there being torn apart by the wind and the rain. I knew I had to go to him.

I didn't say a word to anyone. I sneaked down the cellar stairs and out the door. The rain was coming so hard it hurt. I had to squint to see at all, and I couldn't see much. The wind made things howl and crack.

All I cared about was Hambone, out there with nobody to help. I wondered where the oak tree hit.

There was more lightning, and thunder cracked right after. The storm was on top of us. I thought with each flash and crack that if it hadn't got Hambone this time, it would get him the next. I couldn't get there fast enough.

"Lightning!" I cried. "Lightning! It's me, Jeremy. Strike me dead, lightning, strike me dead. But leave old Hambone alone. He's a memorial now, and he can't die again!"

Suddenly I could see Hambone. I could see his chicken-wire cage every time the sky lighted up. I was nearly there. Hambone looked okay, but I could hardly believe my eyes. I sat down by the cage and began to talk, real fast at first because I was scared and talking kept me from shaking.

"It's okay, Hambone. It's me, Jeremy. Nothing is going to happen to you now, so you don't need to be scared. You're big and strong and there isn't any storm that's going to hurt you. It'll be over soon, and then you can grow and grow. I'm here, Hambone. It's me, Jeremy. Jeremy's here."

I stopped for a moment, but only to catch my breath. Then I kept on talking. It was making me less scared, and I guessed it was making Hambone less scared, too.

"Do you remember when I'd brush you every morning and scratch your belly? You loved to have your belly tickled. You snorted and grunted and rolled on your back in the mud. Remember? And I'd have to brush you all over again. Papa'd yell at me to hurry up, but I'd be laughing so hard I could hardly hear him.

"Sometimes I went to your pen after supper in the summer, when it was still light. I did my spelling, and wrote pretend letters to Mama. You never knew Mama. Just as well, I guess. She didn't like pigs much.

"Mama didn't like much about the farm. It's not her fault, I suppose. At least that's what Stoner says. But I wish she'd known it before.

"Do you think I'll be a farmer, Hambone? I don't mean as good as Papa or Alec. Maybe I can just be a little farmer."

As I talked, the storm began to move away, like storms always do.

Hambone was okay, I could tell it. I could feel it, inside. I lay down beside him in the wet dirt because suddenly I was very tired.

The next thing I knew, I saw Stoner looking at me through the darkness. Then Papa bent down beside me.

"Those aren't tears, Papa," I said to him. "It's the rain."

But the rain had stopped and Papa's face was wet, too. And Stoner's.

Papa pulled a comb from his back pocket. It was Hambone's bone-toothed comb that I had forgotten to bury.

"Stoner said I should bring this out," he said. "She said we could bury it in the dirt around the plant."

I rubbed the comb against my cheek and sank it deep into the wet soil.

Papa carried me into the house and took off my wet clothes. Ramona rubbed me hard with a towel.

"Stoner told you about the plant?" I asked Papa. "That it was a memorial to Hambone?"

"Yep."

"You mad?"

Papa was quiet for a minute. Then he said, "Jeremy, I don't care who you named the plant after. What I care about most is you." Then

he smiled and shook his head. "What I care about next is... that's the biggest tomato plant I've ever seen. The biggest. And probably the only one to make it through this storm. No, I'm not mad. But you scared us all half to death. Next time, you tell me."

Papa carried me up the back stairs to my bed. I looked at the wall behind my head and saw Pridey looking down.

"Mama gave me that," I said to Papa.

"I know," he whispered. "Go to sleep."

picked a hundred and thirty-seven to-matoes from Hambone three weeks after the big storm, and more after that. Everyone said they couldn't get over it, so many tomatoes from one plant.

"It's impossible!" said the reporter from the *Valley Voice*. But he carried a long story about Hambone, with three pictures. It filled two pages.

Papa called us to the fireplace the night the paper came out, and read the article out loud. I lay on my back with my head in Ramona's lap.

When he had finished, he turned to me and said, "I think you should clip this. I think you should send this to your Mama."

"But if I send it to Mama, then I can't paste it on my wall."

Papa pointed to the coffee table in front of the couch. There was a pile of *Valley Voice*s as tall as ten stacks of Sunday pancakes.

Ramona laughed at my surprise and my head bounced up and

down on her stomach.

"Do you think she'd read it?" I asked Papa.

"Yep. She might even paste it to her own wall."

"Okay, I'll send it," I said. "Mama never got to meet Hambone."

Mr. Chamberlain had pasted the story to his counter when we went the next day for milk replacer.

"He's got your touch," Mr. Chamberlain told Papa. "How'd he do it?"

Papa told him to speak to me. "Jeremy's the gardener," he said. I just grinned.

Papa said when the first frost came, "Take the old plant out now. Cut it up and put it back in the hole for next year. And dig some manure into it now. That plant might grow even bigger!"

I looked at Papa and laughed.

I didn't say anything out loud, but I said to myself, "Hambone will live forever."

48